Swimming for Shore in a Sea of Sharks

Joseph McLean Hesh

NAVPRESS

A MINISTRY OF THE NAVIGATORS
P.O. BOX 6000, COLORADO SPRINGS, COLORADO 80934

The CROSSROADS Series Leader's Guide, a helpful one-volume guide for group leaders, is available from NavPress, and covers all four junior high discussion guides:
What's the Big Idea?
Swimming for Shore in a Sea of Sharks
Is My Family Crazy, or Is It Me?
Under the Influence

The Navigators is an international Christian organization. Jesus Christ gave His followers the Great Commission to go and make disciples (Matthew 28:19). The aim of The Navigators is to help fulfill that commission by multiplying laborers for Christ in every nation.

NavPress is the publishing ministry of The Navigators. NavPress publications are tools to help Christians grow. Although publications alone cannot make disciples or change lives, they can help believers learn biblical discipleship, and apply what they learn to their lives and ministries.

Printed in the United States of America

CONTENTS

INTRODUCTION
*Swimming for Shore
in a Sea of Sharks*

Life is like a totally scary ocean full of sharks and barracudas and killer whales and killer seaweed. . . . But there's also friendly stuff, like angelfish and mermaids and Flipper and lobster tails. . . . Hey, there's a lot you can really like about life, but there's plenty to watch out for, too.

So, what's the best way to swim through this gigantic ocean of life? Does the person next to you have it figured out? How about the dude who parties every night of the week? Or the guy with a houseful of nice material things? Or the people who always look good—and know it? Or how about the cool dude who doesn't let all this "God stuff" hassle him? Or the sassy teens who don't give a rip about anybody or anything? Or the guy who just goes wherever the tide takes him?

The goal is to get to shore. But just doing the doggie paddle with the nearest school of cool catfish isn't necessarily going to get you where you may want to go.

EVERYBODY HAVE FUN TONIGHT!
Getting Beyond the Pursuit of Pleasure

◆ICEBREAKER
(Getting your brain in gear)

List the top ten things that teens do at parties. Vote on which three you consider to be the most fun.

◆TUNE IN
(Checking out the situation)

"Matt, you've just got to come. It's gonna be a great party," Bob pleads. Now, Matt is definitely on Bob's "cool" list. But Bob's definition of a "good party" doesn't exactly square with Matt's. The last party that Bob thought was going to be the "social event of the season" was chips 'n' dip and pin the tail on the donkey.

Matt can't help rolling his eyes just at the thought of going to another one of Bob's "biggies" and yet he's in kind of an awkward situation. Matt's mom and Bob's mom are best friends. Matt's mom often pushes him out the door to Bob's house — whether he likes it or not.

"So, Matt, are you coming tonight? Can I expect you?" Matt tries to avoid answering by asking those cool questions that everybody asks when invited to a "questionable" party. "Uh, what are we gonna do?" This is not an unfair question to ask. As you have already figured out, our hero wants to know if it's going to be fun or not. Fun is a key factor . . . particularly when Bob has a track record of chips 'n' dip and pin the tail on the donkey.

Teens have always been interested in fun, and they often prioritize their schedules with fun in mind. Fun is a big social deal, too, because you don't want to show up on Monday morning having been "out-funned" by your locker partner. Bob continues to try really hard to convince Matt that it's gonna be a great night. Matt has to admit that Bob is working hard to make the evening a real hit.

So, Matt sails right into question two, the inevitable and ever-popular, "Who's gonna be there?" You see, diehard *funners* know that human beings can endure incredible things if the right people are doing it! Once again, Matt has asked a fair (and probably smart) question. I mean, who wants to tell about going to a "semi-fun" evening if only "semi-cool" people are in the place?

Now, if Bob has done his homework, he has

a whole bunch of people coming to the deal. Bob appears to be the hardworking, organizing type. And even though he might not always have the coolest friends, he means well and tries hard. Still, to swing Matt, Bob is going to have to have all his ducks in a row. Matt will sacrifice fun if the right people are coming. But . . . if Bob hasn't drawn the right people to the party, then it had better be fun, or else! I mean, after all, it's cooler to be bored sitting at home, right?

◆JUMP IN
(Putting yourself in someone else's shoes)

1. Describe how you think Bob feels trying to "sell" Matt on his party.

2. Describe how Matt feels trying to decide whether or not he's coming to the party.

3. Have you ever felt "forced" into a relationship that didn't come naturally? Explain how that made you feel.

4. Why is "fun" so important at a party?

5. Why do some people feel that they would sacrifice "fun" if the right people are there?

6. What things make a party fun to you?

7. Bob could have better success at parties if he:

   a. stopped playing dorky games like "pin the tail on the donkey." ❑
   b. stopped leaning on Matt and just went his own way. ❑
   c. went to other people's parties for a while. ❑
   d. worked with young children who appreciated his games! ❑
   e. other ________________________.

◆TIME OUT
(Looking at it from another point of view)

Bumper stickers can be good or bad. They can show that the driver has a sharp wit, or they can show that the driver has the brains of a grapefruit. One of the most grapefruit-brained bumper stickers I have ever seen is the famous classic: *If it feels good, do it.* This is the motto of people who are pursuing personal pleasure at whatever price. If it feels good to you, then have sex before marriage. If it feels good to you, shout out a cuss word in public.

Of course, you see that if this slogan goes too far by eliminating *all* boundaries, then how about, If it feels good to you, blow up your school, kill innocent children, slaughter whales and elephants, cut off your arms!!!

A common attitude today is that it's gotta be fun to be done. A person with this kind of attitude will fight work, discipline, and accomplishment. In the end this approach will never satisfy. In a day and age when synthesizers can do so much—when we have electronic rhythm sections in recording studios, cranking out number-one hits—there still remains no substitute for the talent that is carefully crafted through lessons, sweat, and work.

No, work doesn't always feel good. It isn't always fun. But that's just the point. "Fun" in and of itself will never satisfy. Fun is a quick fix, a roller coaster ride that demands another one after it's done. Fun cannot produce in the long haul. It looks good, it feels good, but then it ends, and it has to be reproduced again and again. Fun is truly a good thing only when it's part of a balanced life.

◆GET INTO IT
(Making the situation your own)

1. What do you think of the bumper sticker, "If It Feels Good, Do It"?

   a. Hey, I just don't like bumper stickers, period! ❑

   b. Actually, I don't object to it. It says what I really feel. ❑

   c. There has to be more to life than just fun. ❑

   d. Uh . . . this is a trick question, right? Am I supposed to say something spiritual, or what? ❑

   e. Other ________________________ .

2. Name some things that you do that you know you *need* to do, but that are not all that fun. Why do you continue to do these things?

3. Do you agree that fun is a fake that can't produce in the long haul? Why or why not?

4. In John 10:10 we find that Jesus is promising real "life" to all His followers. He says, "I have come that they may have life, and have it to the full." How does fun fit in there?

5. Why do you think some kids don't apply themselves or give up completely on things like music lessons, school work, or sports training? Do you ever hear stories about people who wished they had stuck with it?

◆A WORD FROM GOD
(Getting the right message)

He who loves pleasure will become poor; whoever loves wine and oil will never be rich. (Proverbs 21:17)

◆FOR THE ROAD
(Taking something along with you)

Explain what fun is in a "balanced life." If Matt was living that balanced life, how would he respond to Bob?

JUST A LITTLE BIT MORE
Getting Beyond the Material World

◆ICEBREAKER
(Getting your brain in gear)

Divide your group in half. Half of the group gets a large amount of play money. The other half goes without. The bills are distributed evenly among the team that has the money. Then they get to "bid" on different items, like cars, planes, etc. After the game, describe how you enjoyed it. Did it make any difference which team you were on—the one with the money or the one without?

◆TUNE IN
(Checking out the situation)

For most of us, extreme poverty means "It's Friday night, and I'm broke." I mean, we're talking serious need here. You're already three allowances behind, no babysitting gigs in sight. Besides, you're a guy. You hate babysitting!

So you stumble up to your room, jump on the bed, and stare out the window. "Can life possibly be this bad?" Your stomach starts to grumble. You look at the digital clock. It's 4:30 in the afternoon. Dad doesn't get home until 6:00, so supper is 90 minutes away.

Oh, the torture. The pain. The torment. You can't take it anymore! You run down the hallway like a madman. Food . . . food! You've got to eat *something*! Your mother sees you at the bottom of the stairs. She has seen that tormented look in your eyes before. She just stands back. You barrel into the kitchen and pull open the refrigerator door . . . and . . . just start eating everything in sight. A pound of bologna . . . leftover pie . . . lasagna . . . a box of baking soda. . . .

WAIT!!!!!! We were talking about poverty, weren't we? You have a refrigerator . . . you have bologna . . . golly, you have a mom! There is something wrong with this picture.

Let me walk you back in time to 1976. Okay, so you weren't even born then. Hang on. It's another one of those "Back when I was your age . . ." stories, so get out the pillows and start yawning.

My wife and I were living in and working for the great state of Mississippi. We were renting a house by the railroad tracks. Each morning at 2:00 a.m., the Illinois Central came barreling through on its way to the Gulf of Mexico. Our house would start to shake whenever the train rolled by. There was a silver trailer parked next door, and the headlight of this massive train would reflect off the trailer right into our bedroom. I know of no horror movie available today that can produce the terrorizing effect of a train driving right into your bed . . . EVERY MORNING AT 2 AM!!!!!!!

Where were we? Oh, yeah, we worked for the state, so we got paid once a month. And even though my wife and I were both working a 40-hour week, the paychecks just didn't seem to stretch far enough. I remember one month when we had absolutely zippo for the entire final week.

So this was poverty, right? Wrong! We still had resources . . . lunch cards at the school cafeteria, a line of credit at the local store, a car that I could have sold (if anyone would have bought it!), and peanut butter in the cupboard. We could have taken on another evening job if things got too tough. We also had families who could help bail us out if we needed help.

Hey! I could go on and on and on. But the point is that this was *not* poverty! You may never experience a standard of living quite that low. And there's a good chance that you'll never even see *real* poverty—people who are homeless, people who are starving, people with no options left.

◆ JUMP IN
(Putting yourself in someone else's shoes)

1. Pretend you wake up one morning and your family discovers there is absolutely no money at all. No savings. No nothing! What would you and your family do?

2. If you lived in a culture where you had to work to help pay the bills, what work do you think you'd be doing?

3. List your resources, kind of like I did above. Which of these do you take for granted?

4. A friend of mine decided to do an experiment one weekend. To prepare for it, he didn't shave for a week, went down to Goodwill and chose the rattiest of clothing items. Then he wandered down to a Gospel Mission to live like someone who was down and out. He slept there. He ate there. He worked the morning shift at the loading dock. The following night, he didn't go back to the mission, but tried a night of sleeping on the street. It was summertime, so he survived okay. List the things you think he might have experienced that you would find it hard to endure.

◆TIME OUT
(Looking at it from another point of view)

One summer I was part of a youth missions trip that spent three weeks in Africa. We built a church, spoke to the people about our faith, and observed miracle after miracle. We also saw poverty—kids without shoes, people working for $5 a day.

WAIT! This isn't poverty, either! They had jobs. They made enough to eat, they fed their families. It was a standard of living quite below where *our* kids were at, but they were maintaining.

So, I watched carefully as I asked the question, "Are they content?" There seemed to be a simple happiness among the people of this African nation, something I don't see a lot of in America. As we sat during their July 5th festival (that was *their* independence day), we heard them sing songs of joy for their president, their country, their everything. They seemed to be happy campers in an overpopulated and relatively poor land. Were they "content"? Well, they certainly appeared to have greater contentment than Americans.

But these people still desired the same kind of things that we want: a larger house, a motor vehicle (Americans want Porsches. They were happy to dream about bicycles that would get them to work and back). Were they truly content? Well, is anyone? Or are we all doomed to always want more, no matter how much we have?

We tend to think of our futures in terms of the financial and material dreams we have, not sure of what we want to do with life itself, but quite aware that we need to keep the party alive. Are *we* content? No. You and I live lives that demand more. Our possessions tell our stories. New clothes. New gadgets to tell others about. New fads. New toys under the Christmas tree. And no matter where we travel in this life, the lack of contentment kicks in our stomachs and tells us that we just gotta have more to be satisfied.

Years ago, a great king wrote a book about what he had found out about life. He wrote about trying to have every pleasure and material possession that money could buy. He concluded that when a person is not content with life, then life basically is a waste of time.

This king named Solomon went on to say that God is the key to true contentment: "Without [God], who can eat or find enjoyment?" (Ecclesiastes 2:25).

◆GET INTO IT
(Making the situation your own)

1. When you look at your current situation in life, how would you describe yourself? (Check just one.)

    a. Perfectly content with all I have, with no desire to have more or get more. ❑
    b. Kind of content with what I have, but a Ferrari in the driveway would be nice. ❑
    c. Mildly content with what I have, so I want to have a job that produces bigger bucks when I get older. ❑
    d. Not really content. Nope. I definitely want *more* in life. ❑
    e. Ticked off. I've been robbed, and now I want to bust out and get the best that life has to offer. ❑

2. What things do you "dream" about owning? Do you really think a day will come when you will own these things?

3. The American Dream has been to give your kids more in life than you have. What do you hope to have that your parents didn't? What do you hope your kids will have that you don't?

4. Describe how you feel, knowing that you have a home, but that there are those in our country and in our world that don't.

5. You have been given $1,000,000. What would you do with the money?

6. Jesus said, "No one can serve two masters. Either he will hate the one and love the other, or he will be devoted to the one and despise the other. You cannot serve both God and Money" (Matthew 6:24). Why do you think we can't serve God and at the same time have a driving desire for more money and the things it can buy?

◆A WORD FROM GOD
(Getting the right message)

People who want to get rich fall into temptation and a trap and into many foolish and harmful desires that plunge men into ruin and destruction. For the love of money is a root of all kinds of evil. (1 Timothy 6:9-10)

◆FOR THE ROAD
(Taking something along with you)

List your ten most important possessions. Number them in order of importance. How many of these are essential to your life? If you gave them all away, who would you give them to? Could life go on without them?

3

MIRROR, MIRROR, ON THE WALL

Getting Beyond a Focus on Self

◆ICEBREAKER
(Getting your brain in gear)

Yucch! As messy as this sounds, collect some eggs, break them as if you were going to fry them in a frying pan, and then have some teens in teams try to glue them back together.

◆TUNE IN
(Checking out the situation)

Picture a giant egg, shattered in a zillion pieces, with an army of king's men trying with Elmer's Glue to make an egg out of all these pieces of shell. Humpty Dumpty took the big dive. And now you have to get together with some of your best friends, a case of Coca Cola, and a bag of pretzels, toss a video in the VCR, and then all sit down and make an egg out of a huge pile of broken shell.

Now, the key phrase in the rhyme is that they just "couldn't put Humpty together again." Now, out of that phrase, which scenario do you picture?

a. An egg crying out in pain from being all cracked up, who will stop crying once all the glue is in place.

b. An egg whose personality has ceased to exist until he is assembled again. (Wow. Sounds like outer space, you know?)

c. An egg who actually is dead, but it was the least that the army could do to assemble this dude for his funeral.

d. "Putting together again" actually means assembling an omelette. Humpty was history, and the soldiers were hungry!

Okay, so you never took a nursery rhyme quite that seriously before! You think that I'm making more out of this story than what it's "cracked up" to be!

Let's look at this from a whole new point of view. If you've ever seen a china doll, you know that on the outside you have this beautiful porcelain doll, but if you were to drop it off the roof of a five-story building, it would fall to the ground and shatter. By the time you got to the bottom floor, the doll would be nowhere to be found . . . just ceramic remains of what used to be a beautiful object.

So what's the point? Each year, American teens spend billions of dollars making the outside of the doll look good. We put cream on our faces, jeans on our legs, and gel in our hair just to keep this outside image intact. Impressions are important. We've learned from advertising that we need to look the part . . . even if we aren't really living it. We have to put on a happy face—even when we're living with a crying heart. Right?

◆JUMP IN
(Putting yourself in someone else's shoes)

1. Which do you spend the most time doing?

    a. Getting dressed in the morning. ❑
    b. Getting dressed to go out at night. ❑
    c. Sitting alone and just thinking through your problems. ❑
    d. Talking seriously about where you are in life. ❑

2. Why do you think the American teen today spends so much money on clothing and makeup?

3. If you're considering asking someone to go out on a date with you, it's most important that that person (choose only one):

    a. look attractive. ❑
    b. fit well with your personality. ❑
    c. have a good reputation. ❑
    d. be a Republican. ❑
    e. like the same music that you like. ❑
    f. really want to go out with you, not just want to use you. ❑

4. Why do teens not feel the "freedom" to act like they really feel?

5. Name a friend you feel you can "be yourself" with. How does that person respond to you on a "bad" day?

◆TIME OUT
(Looking at it from another point of view)

We had a girl visit our youth group one day. She was sort of plain looking . . . nothing particularly unique about her . . . and she blended into the environment rather quickly . . . so much so that she quickly disappeared out the door, and our group didn't hear from her again. Until one of our moms checked with her mom on how things were going, and why the family hadn't been back to church. "Oh, Danielle said that no one in the youth group talked to her." When I inquired of the kids in our group, they all seemed concerned, and yet no one stepped forward that day to do anything about it.

During that week, something unique happened. Several kids in the group wanted to come in and see me because of personal turmoil they were experiencing at that time. It suddenly dawned on me that when someone is focusing on his own needs, he can't see the needs of others.

A key reason why so many people are seeing counselors today is because our society is groomed to *focus on its own problems*. We are acutely aware of our own hurts, just like when we stub our toe or slam our hand in the car door. We run around the streets advertising our own emotional pain. It's no wonder we don't reach out to others to help them in their problems.

The funny thing is that plugging into others and serving them can give us the satisfaction we inwardly hunger for. When our eyes turn inward, we lose sight of the needs of others. The painful truth is that we're either concerned with our own needs or with the needs of Jesus Christ. It's a mighty painful thing for the teen who is caught in the whirlpool of self-concern!

◆GET INTO IT
(Making the situation your own)

1. Why do you think teens are "self-centered" today?

2. At a party, the last thing you think about is:

    a. how you are getting home. ❑
    b. whether or not you're having a good time. ❑
    c. someone who doesn't seem to be having a good time. ❑

    d. when you're going to get to play "pin the tail on the donkey." ❏

    e. why the host isn't playing classical music. ❏

    f. other ________________________ .

3. Describe a time when you put someone else's interests before your own.

4. Can you think of someone in your school who is genuinely concerned for your welfare rather than his or her own?

5. In the story just told, describe what you think Danielle thinks about the youth group. If you were in that youth group, what would you do to change Danielle's mind?

◆ A WORD FROM GOD
(Getting the right message)

Do nothing out of selfish ambition or vain conceit, but in humility consider others better than your-selves. Each of you should look not only to your own interests, but also to the interests of others. (Philippians 2:3-4)

◆ FOR THE ROAD
(Taking something along with you)

If you wanted to start caring more about others, describe how your day's schedule would change tomorrow and what your life would be like.

A REAL COOL DISEASE
Getting Beyond Superficial Faith

◆ICEBREAKER
(Getting your brain in gear)

List some "Christian" activities that you could do on a regular basis yet still not know God.

◆TUNE IN
(Checking out the situation)

Pete was the kind of Christian teen everyone liked. He was tall, good-looking, came from a respected home, had tons of brothers and sisters, athletic ability. . . . Oh, you know the type. The kind of guy most of us used to just sit around and watch and hate inside—wanting to be like him or be liked by him, or even noticed by him.

Well, Pete was kind of a celebrity in the youth group he attended. And, you have to understand my temptation. When you want to do something significant in a community you have to go after the leaders. One look at Pete and you'd say this dude was the best possible leader in the whole group. He said that he believed in Christ. He was a youth group shaker and mover—always there and willing to help. He was a shoo-in to be the class president, both in the church group and in school.

Who wouldn't want to make things happen with a guy like Pete at the front of the parade? In fact, one leader in our church said, "If you can't get Pete, then you might as well throw in the towel." Through further conversations with this man, I discovered that if I didn't get Pete, my job might even be in jeopardy as a youth pastor. I sat down one afternoon and considered my options:

a. Create the grooviest program in the world, with Pete as the major teen leader. We'd have Ferrari giveaways, annual trips in December to Jamaica, dates with Vanna White. . . .

b. Pay Pete $7.50 an hour just to come to stuff. Maybe even create a title like "Peer Youth Coordinator."

c. Trade Pete to a more prestigious church for an undisclosed amount of cash, an old bus, and a hot prospect to be named later.

d. Pray that Pete's dad would get transferred to Frostbite Falls, Minnesota.

e. Pass on the responsibility of high school ministry to some other adults so that I could blame its failures on volunteers.

As you can see, this was a pretty weird situation. And I sometimes wonder how Pete endured the pressure from all corners that he received. In fact, you can pretty much imagine how the church and the neighborhood reacted when one day everybody found out that Pete was admitted to a hospital for drug abuse. You might think this would be the end to the problem, but it was only the beginning. Why? Because what followed in Pete's footsteps was an entire generation of "churched" teens who knew all the right answers but who lived a life that was not much different from the lives of teens who never even heard about Jesus.

◆ JUMP IN
(Putting yourself in someone else's shoes)

1. Hey, is this really possible? How could Pete's problem go unnoticed by so many for so long?

2. If you wanted to reach your school through the student leadership, name five kids that you would target.

3. What does Pete's behavior tell you about the youth program he was involved in?

4. Some kids felt threatened by Pete and wouldn't get near him—or even try. Why do you think this was the case? Can you think of anyone in your school like Pete?

◆TIME OUT
(Looking at it from another point of view)

"The real disease." I like that phrase. I've forgotten who said it to me first. It was a way of describing people who are "for real" with God; people who really know Jesus and love Him; people who are Christians—no doubt about it. They have the real condition, the real disease called Christianity. They walk the talk.

The people who have this rather cool spiritual disease may not look "cool" on the surface, but they usually show certain signs—like being honest, caring about people, not cutting people down, sticking up for what's right. If somebody doesn't show any of these signs, it makes you wonder if they're for real with God, if they *really* believe in Him or if they're just giving God the silent treatment.

Christians aren't always "the beautiful people" like Pete. Guys like Pete can often turn it on and turn it off at just the right time. And Christians aren't necessarily the kids from Christian families. Some of those "churched" kids know all the answers, but don't show any of the life.

It's not always that easy to pick out these teens with this cool kind of disease, because sometimes they resemble nerds and sometimes they're last year's hell-raisers. Some are in the choir and some are football players. But there's something in common that links them all: *Their God is not silent.*

Now this doesn't mean that they have a holy glow or that they have to take their Bible to school . . . but they sure take their faith to school. And their relationship with Jesus doesn't stay in their locker. Jesus would call this cool kind of disease "really living" (John 10:10). It's the life He intended us all to have . . . and it goes far beyond just the outward show. There is stuff *inside* that is real about "the real disease."

◆GET INTO IT
(Making the situation your own)

1. What's the difference between Pete and a person with "the real disease"?

2. Describe what you think the real disease feels like.

3. Is God capable of creating the real disease in you? How do you know?

4. How can a Christian teen be "really living" the way Jesus described (John 10:10) and yet have a crummy home life, or have things going wrong at school?

◆ A WORD FROM GOD
(Getting the right message)

"Not everyone who says to me, 'Lord, Lord,' will enter the kingdom of heaven, but only he who does the will of my Father who is in heaven." (Matthew 7:21)

◆ FOR THE ROAD
(Taking something along with you)

Think about the people closest to you. Then make a list of the ones who have "the real cool disease."

5

APOCALYPSE TOMORROW
Getting Beyond Despair and Rebellion

◆ICEBREAKER
(Getting your brain in gear)

Take a quick look at a recent newspaper. Find one piece of good news and one piece of bad news.

◆TUNE IN
(Checking out the situation)

Some of the horror stuff we're exposed to today can keep us awake at night. Why, just the television commercials about upcoming movies about weird dudes with long fingernails, hockey masks, or chainsaws, and beasties jumping out of people's stomachs, little girls walking into TV sets. . . . Hey, we're talking strange stuff, eh?

But, there is a horror that's even worse, and it's on prime time TV. Sounds weird, doesn't it? No, I'm not talking about Saturday morning cartoons, although they have some stuff on there that looks like it went through a trash compactor first. No, that horror of horrors . . . that fear of fears . . . that yecchh of yecchhs . . . is the (are you sure you are ready for this?) the NEWS!!!

I think I hear the groans of unbelievers out there. Okay, let me build my case. I think when it's over, you'll agree. As I write this, the city of San Francisco has just suffered one of the worst disasters of the decade: an earthquake causing many deaths, injuries, and billions of dollars worth of damage. The TV screen keeps showing footage of a car driving off a section of a bridge—and it isn't a stunt man driving. This isn't the world of pretend, where you shoot the scene over and over again and no one gets hurt. This is real people in real trauma . . . real people really dying.

Disaster and death get beaten into you on a regular basis in daily news reports, special news bulletins, and "investigative" news shows that go behind the scenes. You find yourself watching the same footage, watching the same people cry the same tears—tears that don't stop when the director yells "Cut!" Doesn't it sometimes frighten you that *you* could have been the one in the accident, the one in the middle of a real living nightmare?

Okay, I admit that the news serves a purpose. It tells me a lot about my world. What the news doesn't tell me is what to do with all this cruddy information. Sure, I'm learning all about my world. But *what a world!* Tragedy after tragedy after tragedy, most of us develop a glaze around our hearts to keep from developing "news nightmares."

You'll notice that the TV news anchors don't really smile a whole lot—unless they end their newscast with some funny story about a potato museum or singing dogs. And small wonder!

There's just not a whole lot of news to smile about! Not much seems to be optimistic . . . which has to puzzle people who believe in the evolution of our species. Nothing seems to be "getting better." There's always a new war, new rumors of war, people exposed for their sin and greed and corruption. There are always new names, but it's still the same old stuff.

Now, here's the bitter conclusion of all this: I believe that suicide is a result of a person waking up in the morning and seeing bad news on every wall—when there's no check in the mail, when we run out of dreams, when there's no warm, loving cocoon called home that will embrace us, even though the whole world around us appears to be going to hell in a handcart.

I had to explain what my daughter was watching in the San Francisco earthquake footage when she asked, "Daddy, are those people really dead?" And yet, because of the love we experience in our home, she could live through the reality. Suicide sometimes comes when the reality, the tragedy, hurts us more than the love heals . . . and when we listen to negative voices that tell us it's all over, there's no tomorrow, there will be clouds tomorrow with no hope of the sun.

When I once went to visit a family where the father had just taken his own life, I saw looks of utter shock and hopelessness on the faces of the mom and the kids. It's like the day when you hear that your friend just died in a car accident, or that your dad just walked out on your mom. GAG! How do people get on with their lives if they can't know how to plan? If they don't know whether to wait or keep going?

Still not convinced? A news report states that

tens of millions of babies have been aborted since 1973. Homeless people wander the streets of your own town, with no place to sleep tonight. Global destruction of the environment affects the very air we breathe. Fifty percent of today's marriages end up in divorce. The news anchor talks about an assassination in a remote country, with people rioting in the streets. And a report states that an American teenager eats more food in a day than a person in an underdeveloped country may see in a month. And these TV news reports are all about living, sensitive people just like you and me.

So, how in the world can we live with the pressure? How can we live with all this horror? It's easy. Put the weather and sports on after the gory news! After all, that's all we really want to see anyway, right? No rain tomorrow . . . our favorite team won the game . . . and another day goes on. When the news is over, turn on MTV, and no big deal, right?

◆JUMP IN
(Putting yourself in someone else's shoes)

1. How do you react to the stuff that gets reported on the news?

2. Do you believe that television has increased the amount of stress that we feel? Why or why not?

3. What type of news story bothers you the most?

    a. Large-scale disaster. ❑
    b. Murder. ❑
    c. Airplane crash. ❑
    d. People dying from eating a kind of food you like. ❑
    e. An endangered species. ❑
    f. The homeless and the poor. ❑

4. How much does television influence the way you live your life?

    a. A little. ❑
    b. Just average. ❑
    c. A lot. ❑
    d. It's my number-one influence. ❑

◆TIME OUT
(Looking at it from another point of view)

Suicide . . . a private apocalypse. Newsmen covering a suicide never give you the picture of a brighter tomorrow. You don't just look at a family in pain and say, "Everything's gonna work out fine for them." Do we even have a clue when it comes to suicide? Can anyone really help people who are caught up in this dark private pool of soul-wrenching pain?

Yes. God can help. The Bible talks about a time when there will be no more tears, no more sorrow, no more death and dying. It talks about hanging on to God through all the horrors and tragedies of this life. God explains in His Word about the spiritual sickness of sin, and how to reach out to someone in pain. It is *God* who gives us something concrete in a world of Jell-O.

If Jesus Christ is not the answer to stop people

from committing suicide, from that personal apocalypse of self-destruction, then I have nothing else to offer. Money, knowledge, power, sex—none of these things can satisfy that emptiness deep inside. It would be like you coming to my drugstore for a cure for some sickness and finding an empty shelf. There is nothing apart from Jesus Christ that can solve the problems and the sickness of a world full of bad news.

◆GET INTO IT
(Making the situation your own)

1. Why do you believe that suicide is such an attractive option for some teenagers?

2. Describe your home life. (You can check more than one.)

    a. A warm cocoon of love. ❑
    b. A fun place to be. ❑
    c. Sometimes good and sometimes not. ❑
    d. A place I would rather avoid. ❑
    e. A negative scene. ❑

3. What would you tell a friend whose father had committed suicide?

4. What would you say to convince a friend not to commit suicide?

5. Read Psalm 42:5. What kinds of feelings are expressed in this verse?

6. Why do you think a person who seemed to have it all together—good looks, talent, etc.—might try to commit suicide?

◆ A WORD FROM GOD
(Getting the right message)

The LORD is close to the brokenhearted and saves those who are crushed in spirit. (Psalm 34:18)

◆ FOR THE ROAD
(Taking something along with you)

If you were a newscaster and could control how the newscast is done, how would you present some tragic news yet still give a positive point of view?

GO AGAINST THE FLOW
Getting Beyond Shifting Values

◆ICEBREAKER
(Getting your brain in gear)

Pick someone in the group to be president of the United States. Hold a mock news conference. The rest of you will be news reporters and will ask questions of the president. Make sure the president gets some tough questions.

◆TUNE IN
(Checking out the situation)

Is history one of your favorite subjects? Probably not. You might not enjoy having to learn about George Washington and Thomas Jefferson over and over again. I find history more fun and more interesting as I get older, but that doesn't mean that history class was the best show in town when I was in eighth grade.

The first challenge in teaching history to junior

highers, in my opinion, would be to make it inter-esting. That would include field trips, historical reenactments, making huge table maps, making battles come to life, dressing up weird, and doing history in junior high language.

The second challenge would be to know what things to stress and what things to discard. Yes, we all probably memorize more historical dates than we would like to. And years after the course has ended, we still know the dates but we don't have a clue about what happened on those dates. History must become a subject that does more than pre-pare a person for Trivial Pursuit games.

That is why if I were a history teacher, I would stress "people stories." One person I would love to spend a whole day, week, month, or decade on is Daniel Webster. Here are the things you will forget about Daniel Webster:

a. He did not invent the dictionary. (That was *Noah* Webster.)

b. He was not an English drama dude. (That was *John* Webster.)

c. He *was* an American political leader in the early 1800s.

The thing you must not forget about Web-ster is his famous statement, "I'd rather be right than president." I like that. This guy is regular blood and guts, a politician with real commitment. Junior highers are smart. You've already figured out that society knows how to talk out of both sides of its mouth at the same time. A lot of poli-ticians are real good at playing games in order to survive. That's why I believe Daniel Webster is a real man of honesty and courage. What he was saying was that he would rather be able to face his conscience, rather be able to stick to his guns, than to be in control of the most powerful office in our land.

We tend to admire a guy who isn't scared to do what's right—to show some backbone and to challenge us to do the same. The problem is that you and I don't have a lot of models like this to follow. We live instead in a world where people are almost *expected* to change their mind when political advantage is involved. Instead of facing conflict head-on, most people cower inside the shadow of wanting to please everyone. In essence, they'd rather be president than right.

◆JUMP IN
(Putting yourself in someone else's shoes)

1. Why do you agree or disagree with the statement, "I'd rather be right than president"?

2. Name someone you know who would rather be right than president.

3. Name someone who would rather be president than right!

4. Why do we often choose to take the easy way out rather than facing conflict?

◆TIME OUT
(Looking at it from another point of view)

Does living in a world of abortion bother you? Because of the media influence in our day and age, it's interesting to study what bothers the social conscience of our country. Often I see news stories about the killing of whales. Whales are very near and dear to the American heart, just like pandas. If you did a survey door to door, you'd probably find that nobody wants to see pandas or whales or any other animals wind up with the same fate as passenger pigeons and dodo birds . . . in other words, extinct!

We see stories in the news about many important problems: the plight of starving and homeless people, the pollution of our entire planet, racial discrimination, etc. But it's important to remember that you and I must decide for ourselves what causes we truly consider to be important.

Let's start with the issue of whales. I love whales. Why, some of my best friends . . . no, maybe not. But yes, I get mad when I see television footage of elephants getting blown away. And I am truly sad when I see us consuming a ton of food and materials while the homeless rot in the streets, and while the hungry die the painful death of starvation. And yes, I get bummed when a boy panda and a girl panda can't get together during a romantic fling in a Washington zoo.

But, wait a minute! How is it that a person can watch all this, have his heart jump up in his throat, cry real tears, bang on the table, and be convinced that something has got to change . . . and then completely ignore the fact that millions of babies are being killed in hospitals today? Some people respond, "It's a woman's right to her own body." Well, I suppose what a woman does with *her* body is her business. But isn't there somebody else's body (and life) involved in an abortion? Personally, I don't think it's anybody's "right" to ignore people in need, to blow away elephants, to harpoon an entire species of whales, or to blow away humans who have not yet been born.

We are living in a world that kind of "feels" its way toward what is right or wrong . . . who lives or dies . . . who succeeds and fails . . . who eats and who starves. And this is the world you are growing up into. You will watch television, and what you watch there will probably shape your view of your world. But you will find most of your deepest questions unanswered there.

Don't you just hunger for consistency? Don't you want to see a sense of justice and truth, rather than a country simply making decisions from day to day based on whatever is convenient or popular?

Let's pretend that I, for some incredible reason, get nominated to run for president. As a key to my campaign, I make the Bible my platform. In other words, my decisions about foreign policy, budget, defense, and so on, all flow from the Bible. What do you think the big deals would be? Where should I spend most of my time, energy, and effort? What would my stand on the homeless, saving whales and elephants, and abortion be? Would I come to a time in my administration where I would have to say, "I would rather be right than president," and then resign my administration and walk away, or would I bend my rules, remain president, and then never be able to look in the mirror again?

◆GET INTO IT
(Making the situation your own)

Surprise! You are now a nominee for the office of president of the United States, and you have been asked to give your opinions on the following issues, with the Bible as your "chief advisor" for your task in the next four years. How would you handle the following topics:

a. Relations with the Soviet Union.

b. Relations with terrorists in other countries.

c. Taxes, spending, and the budget.

   d. Environment, ecology, the situation of our nation's resources.

   e. The rights of minorities in our country.

   f. Abortion.

   g. The plight of the starving and homeless.

   h. Women's rights.

◆A WORD FROM GOD
(Getting the right message)

We are not trying to please men but God, who tests our hearts. (1 Thessalonians 2:4)

◆FOR THE ROAD
(Taking something along with you)

As a group, write a letter to the president of the United States. Ask for a brief policy statement in the areas we have mentioned. Perhaps your Congressman can help you. Once you have received the policy statement, talk about it, and give it a biblical review. Answer the question: "Why is it difficult to implement biblical principles in America's government?"